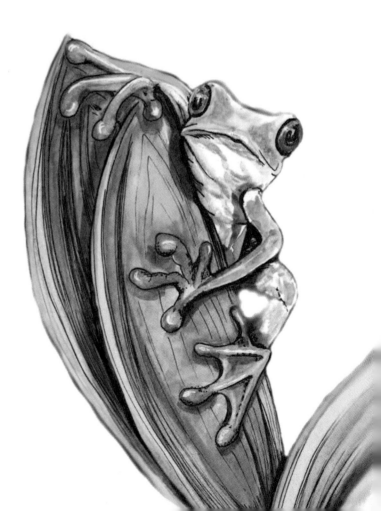

A special thank you
to Daniel,
you have kept us grounded
and reminded us
what the real treasures
in life are.

Little Red-Eyed Tree Frog

Story written by Jessica Patterson

Illustrated by Susan Mayfield

Grown-ups say, you can not see the forest because of all of the trees. This means you cannot see what is in front of your face because you are too busy looking all around you at the smaller details. But sometimes grown-ups get too busy and they forget to look at the tinier things in life beyond their nose. There is a whole world hidden deep in the rainforest jungle between the flowers and leaves.

Tucked under

a hibiscus flower

was Little Red-Eyed Tree Frog,

who lived with his mother.

Little Red-Eyed Tree Frog

spent his days exploring the

plants nearby. He crawled up and down

the vines. He jumped in and out of

the flowers. One day he grumbled,

"There is nothing exciting around here."

His thoughts were interrupted by a thunderous whoosh. He glanced up and saw a fluttering blue cloud swarming through the trees. Thousands and thousands of blue morpho butterflies, invaded his backyard.

His mother greeted one of the butterflies "Welcome back, my friend."

The butterfly said, "Thank you, it is good to be back."

Little Red-Eyed Tree Frog asked
doubtfully, "Why would you
want to come back here?"
The butterfly replied, "We have returned to see
the jewel of the earth once again."
Little Red-Eyed Tree Frog bounced excitedly and
thought, "A jewel! Where is this gem?
I wonder why I have not seen it. I must go
hunt for it."

Little Red-Eyed Tree Frog

climbed down his familiar vine

and jumped across the flowers.

Soon he saw plants he had never

encountered before. He came to

the edge of a pond where he spied a

bright shiny globe floating above the

water.

It glistened like

a jewel. "This must be it! Maybe I can

swim out there and bring it back." He

inched closer to the water and was about

to jump in when he heard a voice behind him

squeal, "I would not go out there if I

were you. He might eat you!"

Up popped Baby Tapir and he said,

"That is a crocodile!"

"But it shines like a jewel,"

replied Little Red-Eyed Tree Frog.

"Oh, no, that is an eye belonging to a crocodile

and I have watched him devour many animals.

Why would you think there was a jewel out

in the water?"

"I heard there was a jewel in the rainforest and I am going to find it," said Little Red-Eyed Tree Frog.

Baby Tapir offered, "I have been digging around here scrounging for tasty treats and I have never discovered a jewel. If I were going to hide something special I would put it up high out of reach."

Little

Red-Eyed Tree Frog

continued his journey and

scrambled up the rainforest canopy. He

met a chameleon and explained

how he was looking for a jewel.

Chameleon said,

"What good is a jewel?

All I need is a big juicy bug."

Without moving a muscle, and

faster than the eye could see,

the chameleon flicked out his

tongue like a whip and gobbled up a

caterpillar that was crawling nearby. He

began to munch. A hummingbird zipped

between the two and zigzagged through

the forest. Little Red-Eyed Tree Frog

decided to follow.

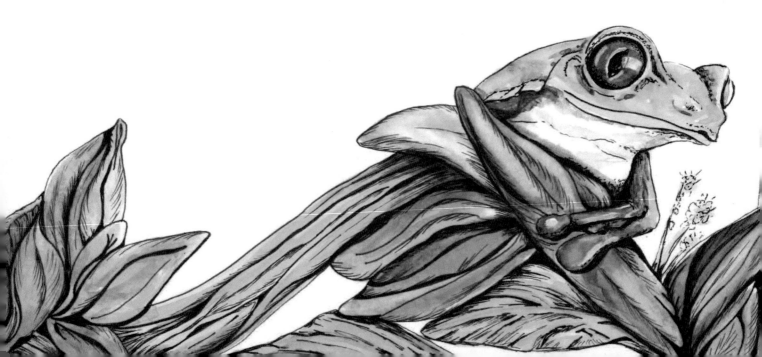

Trying to catch his breath, Little Red-Eyed Tree Frog finally caught up with Hummingbird who was visiting with Mouse Opossum. He asked the pair about a jewel hiding in the forest. Mouse Opossum started to say, "I am not sure about a jewel, but I heard over on the next tree there was..." But he never finished. In fact, in the blink of an eye he and Hummingbird disappeared.

Little Red-Eyed Tree Frog
instantly knew why they left
without another word. There
suddenly appeared an ocelot nosing
around for a tasty treat. The little
tree frog leaped into a snug shelter and
held his breath. He could feel the ocelot's
whiskers brush against the flower
he safely took cover in.

Little Red-Eyed Tree Frog came out to see if the ocelot had left and it was safe to continue. He peeked around a leaf and caught the glimmer of silver rings wrapped around a small branch. Could a jewel be attached to them? He crept closer to get a better look.

No, the rings
were claws
attached to a sleeping
baby sloth. Little Red-Eyed Tree
Frog woke the sloth up and asked
him if he had seen a jewel.
Baby Sloth said, "All that is dear to me
is sleep and lots of fresh berries to eat."

With that he closed his eyes
and began to snooze again.

"SSSSSsleep and berriesSSS."

Little Red-Eyed Tree Frog looked up and saw two yellow-green eyes of a snake curled on a branch inches away staring at him. Wishing he was back at home with his mother, Little Red-Eyed Tree Frog courageously asked the snake about the jewel. Slithering closer, the snake hissed, "Ssssearch elssssewhere."

Calming his nerves and being on the lookout for possible dangers, Little Red-Eyed Tree Frog was pondering where to look next when he heard a voice say, "Mine is more valuable. Behold how brilliant the colors are and they go on forever." "Maybe this is true," said another voice, "but mine is just as colorful. See how large it is, it must be more valuable." "Could they be arguing about jewels?" thought Little Red-Eyed Tree Frog.

Little Red-Eyed Tree

Frog was surprised to find two

birds arguing about whether

Toucan's beak was greater

than Quetzal's long tail. He

tried several times to interrupt to

ask about the jewel he was looking

for, but their voices kept getting

louder and they never noticed

him sitting there at all.

"Hrmph!" came a growl from

above.

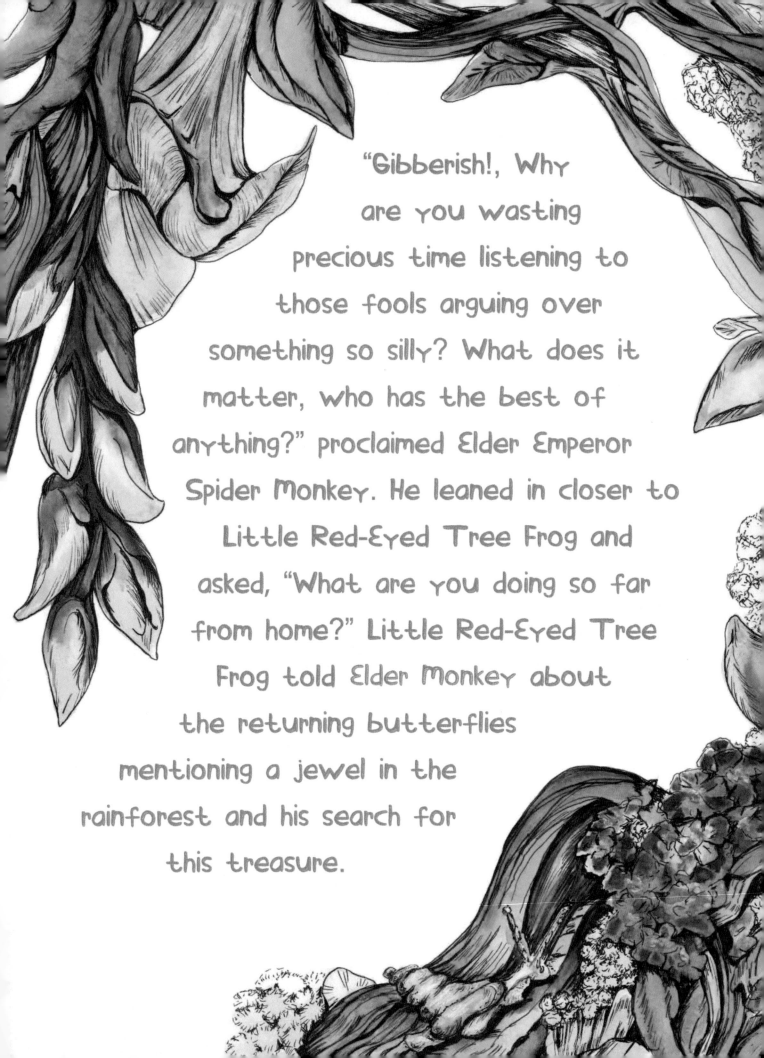

"Gibberish!, Why are you wasting precious time listening to those fools arguing over something so silly? What does it matter, who has the best of anything?" proclaimed Elder Emperor Spider Monkey. He leaned in closer to Little Red-Eyed Tree Frog and asked, "What are you doing so far from home?" Little Red-Eyed Tree Frog told Elder Monkey about the returning butterflies mentioning a jewel in the rainforest and his search for this treasure.

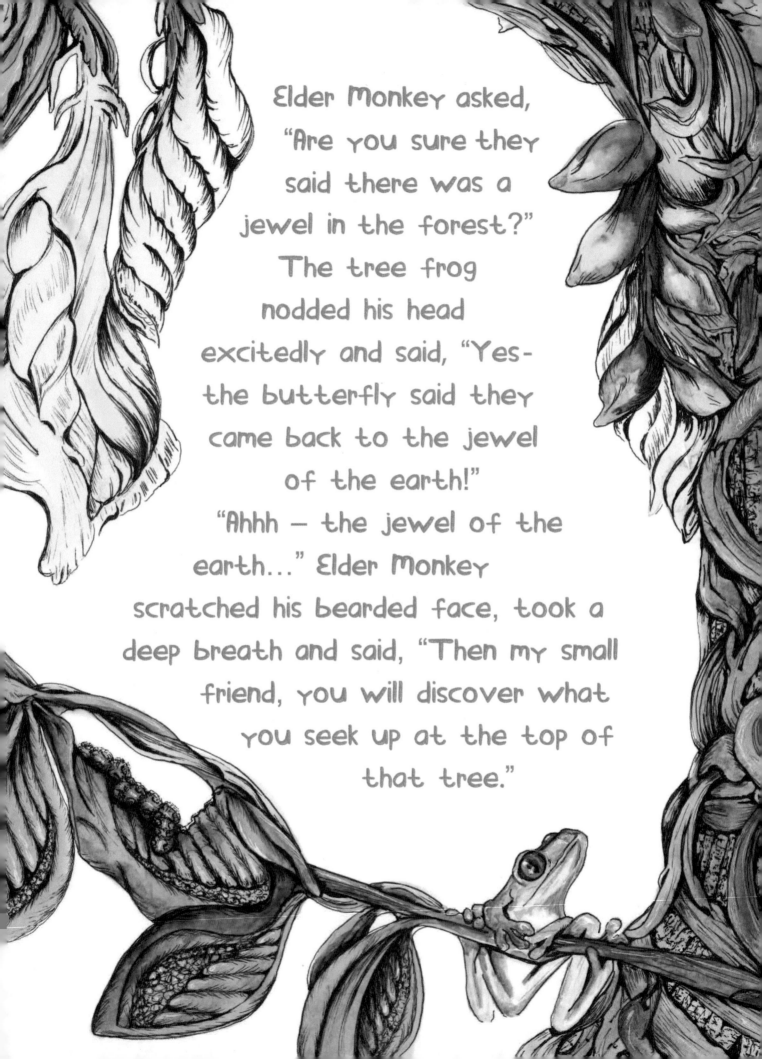

Elder Monkey asked,
"Are you sure they
said there was a
jewel in the forest?"
The tree frog
nodded his head
excitedly and said, "Yes-
the butterfly said they
came back to the jewel
of the earth!"
"Ahhh — the jewel of the
earth..." Elder Monkey
scratched his bearded face, took a
deep breath and said, "Then my small
friend, you will discover what
you seek up at the top of
that tree."

Little Red-Eyed Tree Frog
left Elder Monkey and slowly
began his climb to the top
of the tree. When he reached the
top he found a nest. Relieved to finally
find the jewel, he took a deep breath
and looked inside, but all he saw were
three bird eggs. He was bewildered.

"May I help you?"

Frog turned around to see
Harpy Eagle looking at him.
Little Red-Eyed Tree Frog
stammered and said he was on a
quest to find a jewel. The eagle said,
"These eggs are my family and they
are the most important treasure I
could ever possess."

Little Red-Eyed Tree Frog was so
confused. He hopped out of the nest and
onto the end of a tree branch. He thought,
"Elder Monkey said I would discover the
jewel of the earth at the top of this
tree, but there were only eggs."
Suddenly Little Red-Eyed Tree Frog
saw a whole new world
around him.

The setting sun made
the rainforest canopy
glow like fire. The river glistened like
stars. The beauty took his breath
away. Now he realized what it meant
to not see the forest for the trees.
He had been so busy looking at details
the he never saw the
bigger picture.

The jewel the butterflies talked about was not anything like a diamond. Little Red-Eyed Tree Frog's rainforest was the jewel of the earth.

Stay curious, like Little Red-Eyed Tree Frog. Seek your fortune, but never forget what the real treasures in life are all about.

Protect our rainforest.

Made in the USA
Monee, IL
10 November 2021